398.2   Esbensen, Barbara
ESB   Juster

       Ladder to the sky

   $14.45

Ladder to the Sky

How The Gift of Healing Came to the Ojibway Nation

A Legend Retold by

Barbara Juster Esbensen

Illustrated by

Helen K. Davie

Little, Brown and Company
Boston   Toronto   London

Author's Note

In their own language, the Ojibway, or Chippewa people, are known as Anishinabe—"original people." Because their culture and language are based on stories told, not written down, there are often different versions of the same tale. The one I am telling here is based on the 1850 work by the Ojibway chief Kah-ge-ga-gah-bowh, who later took the name George Copway. In 1850 he wrote a book setting down Ojibway history, customs, and legends because he was afraid this valuable information would one day disappear entirely.

— B.J.E.

First Edition

Ladder to the Sky is an Ojibway legend retold
from *The Traditional History and Characteristic Sketches
of the Ojibway Nation*
by George Copway, Chief of the Ojibway Nation
(London: Charles Gilpin, Publishers, 1850).

Library of Congress Cataloging-in-Publication Data
Esbensen, Barbara Juster.
   Ladder to the sky.

   An Ojibway legend retold from George Copway's Traditional
history and characteristic sketches of the Ojibway nation.
   Summary: Recounts the legend of how the gift of healing
came to the Ojibway people.
   1. Chippewa Indians—Legends. 2. Indians of North
America—Legends. [1. Chippewa Indians—Legends.
2. Indians of North America—Legends] I. Davie, Helen, ill.
II. Copway, George, 1818–1863? Traditional history and
characteristic sketches of the Ojibway nation. III. Title.
E99.C6E7 1988   398.2'08997 [E]   87-22729
ISBN 0-316-24952-1

10 9 8 7 6 5 4 3 2 1

WOR

*Published simultaneously in Canada
by Little, Brown & Company (Canada) Limited*

Printed in the United States of America

In Ojibway words,
our English vowels make these new sounds:

a becomes *ah*   *i* becomes *ee*
e becomes *ay*   and *o* becomes *oh*

Long ago, in the old, forgotten time,
Gitchi Manitou, the Great Spirit, created only
strong, healthy people.

In those days, all the men were tall and brave.
They could run like the storm wind.
In their games, they were clever and swift,
and they knew all the secrets
of the four-legged ones — the forest animals
who were their brothers.

The women in those times sang as they worked.
Their clear voices filled the forest with melodies,
and they walked with light step and straight back,
even when they were very old.
They copied the fragrant flowers
that grew like colored stars
among the grasses. They wove flower shapes
into bright bands to bind their long, black hair.
With nimble fingers,
the women wove the rushes and reeds
into sweet-smelling mats
to cover the floors of their tepees.
They gathered milkweed down
to make soft beds for their babies.

From birch bark they could make a strong container,
a muk-kuk, to fill with all the plenty
of woodland and stream.

Nobody was ever sick
in those days. Nobody died.

When somebody grew old,
Manitou sent one of the shining spirit-messengers
down the magic vine that grew in the very center
of the Ojibway lands.
The vine grew in the earth,
but its far-off top was looped around a star.

The shining spirit-messenger would carry the old one
up and up and up through the vine's great leaves —
up into the sky itself.
There, the old ones lived forever,
watching over their beloved people
and the campfires twinkling below.

The Ojibway people were forbidden to touch
this magic vine.
It was a living ladder connecting the earth
with Manitou's great blue sky home.

Other spirit-messengers also came to earth
from time to time to see
that everything was going well.
These spirits came down the magic vine
from the North, the South, the East, and the West —
from every corner of Gitchi Manitou's kingdom.
They took the form of Indians,
and they would walk through a village or a camp
and speak to every person living there —
no matter how young, no matter how old.

"Are you content?" the spirits would ask.
"Is there anything you need?"
Everyone was treated the same.
In the eyes of the Great Spirit,
all were equal.
But one day, in one of the villages,
discontent began to grow
like a dark thornbush shadow
spreading along the pathways.

... this village,
the people saw that their spirit-messenger
favored a certain young man
who had lived among them all his life
in the lodge of his loving grandmother.

Every time the spirit appeared,
it would invite the young man to walk
arm in arm with it through the village.

Nothing like this had ever happened before.
The people were jealous, and their anger grew.
They feared the spirit,
but they did not fear the young man.
Whenever he was alone, they gathered stones in secret
and shouted insults at the young man.
Sharp stones flew at him from hidden places.

The poor young man was afraid to go about in the village.
But he was afraid to stay in his grandmother's lodge, too.
All night he could hear the sounds of villagers
circling the lodge and muttering threats.
At last, he only wished to leave his village.
He wanted to disappear into the sky
with the spirit messenger.

One day, the spirit appeared in the old woman's lodge
where the sad young man was sitting.
The spirit stretched out its arms.
"Your sad thoughts have reached me.
You shall come with me and live in the kingdom
of Gitchi Manitou, the Great Spirit, forever."

Desperately, the grandmother
tried to clutch her grandson's arm
but before she could touch him or cry out,
the young man was wrapped in a crackling blue light.
It carried him in a flash through the air
and up the magic vine.

The spirit and the young man were gone!

The old woman wailed and shouted
for him to return.
"Be-ga-wain! Be-ga-wain!
Come back! Come back!"
But there was no answer.

When darkness fell on the village,
the grandmother crept along the forest edge
until she reached the forbidden vine.
When she came near the vine,
it began to give off a wild light,
and a force from within it
seemed to be pushing her away.
But old women have a force of their own.
She broke through the power of the vine
and wrapped her arms around its cold stem.

All night she climbed.
The vine swayed and buckled under her weight,
but still she went up and up and up.

When the sun rose, the people awoke
and saw that the old woman's lodge was empty!
They searched everywhere for her.
Where could she be?
Then someone shouted and pointed to the sky.

Ay-e-e-e! The people were horrified.
They could see the old woman,
but she was only a small speck
climbing that forbidden vine
where it nearly touched the sun.

She had disobeyed Gitchi Manitou,
the Great Spirit!
"Be-ga-wain!" they shouted at her.
"Come back!"
The vine rippled and shuddered,
but still she went on.
The vine looked as thin as a hair.
"You old witch!" they screamed.
"Come back!"

"Set fire to her lodge," cried the chiefs.
"She is bringing shame and disaster to us all!"

Now at last,
the old woman was near the top
where the vine was a thin tendril
tied to a star.

Her tired fingers reached out
to pull her weary body
past the star-anchor
and onto the floor of the sky kingdom.

But, after all,
this magic vine was made only
for spirits to use.

SNAP! CRA-A-A-ASH!
A sound like thunder
followed the young man's grandmother
as she plummeted to earth!

The sound was heard in all the villages
in all four corners of the Ojibway forest nation.

And from all four corners,
the people swept in like a great wind
to gather in a circle where the grandmother lay
in the cold ruins of the magic vine.

They pushed and pulled at her.
"What will happen to us now?" they cried.
The grandmother covered her ears
to keep out their angry shouts.
"What punishment have you brought down on us,
you old witch?"

They did not have to wait long for their answer.

Pain and discomfort began to strike
first this one, then that one.
Their legs ached. Their heads hurt.
Some could not walk. Others could not speak.
Some of the people fell to the ground.
They looked like they were asleep,
but they did not move or breathe.

A sorrow and a stillness
hung like a black robe
over all the land.

There was no more singing.
There were no more games.
No longer did the sounds of contented people
soothe the heavy sun to its evening rest.

Now the people understood:
Disease and death were their punishment.
What could they do?

They could only wait.

Then one day,
the air was filled with strange blue lights,
and the spirit-beings came drifting down
out of the sky.
Their faces were sad.
They had no blessings for the people.
They had no gifts.
All the spirits raised their voices together.

"One of you chose to disobey Gitchi Manitou.
Now your punishment is upon you.
From this time forward, disease and pain will live among
your people.

"The sacred vine was always,
from the beginning of all time,
your connection to the sky-kingdom
where you would finally live forever.
The connection has been broken.
Your people will no longer live forever.
Now all must die when their time comes.

"But," the spirits told them,
"Gitchi Manitou has sent us back
to show you how to release your people
from pain and misery.

"Watch!"
And the spirits spread out their arms
until they were filled with all the flowers
and all the growing plants on earth.
These they dried with their warm hands and,
blowing on the leaves and petals,
scattered them again over all the Ojibway lands.

"Gitchi Manitou sends us here to say
that every flower that buds
can serve a wise and healing purpose.
Every blade of grass can be useful.
Growing everywhere around you
are plants that will cure all illnesses
and help all those in pain."
The spirits seemed to be speaking
with one silvery voice.

"You have always woven the supple reeds
into mats for your tepees.
You have always spread your blankets
over fragrant cedar branches and pine boughs.
You have always looked at the delicate flowers
and twisting woodland vines
and copied their shapes and colors
to decorate your clothes.
"But now we will choose from among you
the Mi-di-wi-win — the Grand Medicine People.
We will show the Mi-di-wi-win
the secrets of these plants.
The Mi-di-wi-win will learn to use roots
and petals and stems and leaves
to make you well when you fall sick.

"In their Medicine Lodges,
the Mi-di-wi-win will call out to the Great Spirit.
They will sing their songs
and dance their sacred dances
in honor of these truths.

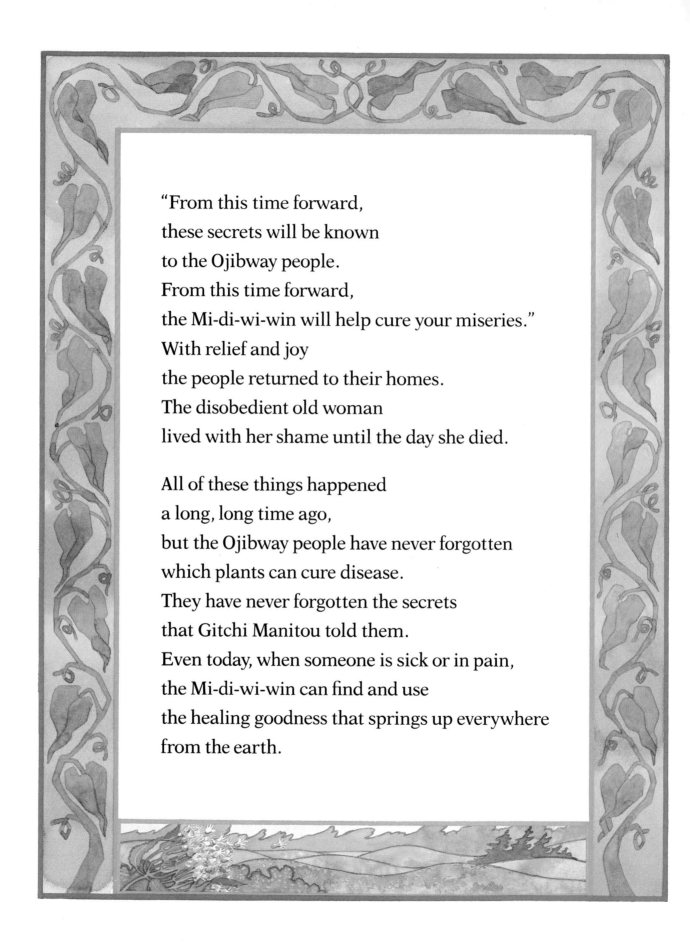

"From this time forward,
these secrets will be known
to the Ojibway people.
From this time forward,
the Mi-di-wi-win will help cure your miseries."
With relief and joy
the people returned to their homes.
The disobedient old woman
lived with her shame until the day she died.

All of these things happened
a long, long time ago,
but the Ojibway people have never forgotten
which plants can cure disease.
They have never forgotten the secrets
that Gitchi Manitou told them.
Even today, when someone is sick or in pain,
the Mi-di-wi-win can find and use
the healing goodness that springs up everywhere
from the earth.